Welcome to ALADDIN QUIX!

If you are looking for fast, fun-to-read stories with colorful characters, lots of kid-friendly humor, easy-to-follow action, entertaining story lines, and lively illustrations, then **ALADDIN QUIX** is for you!

But wait, there's more!

If you're also looking for stories with tables of contents; word lists; about-the-book questions; 64, 80, or 96 pages; short chapters; short paragraphs; and large fonts, then **ALADDIN QUIX** is *definitely f*

ALADDIN QUIX: Tl
to reads and longer, n
books, for readers five ...rs old.

Read more ALADDIN QUIX books!

By Stephanie Calmenson

Our Principal Is a Frog!

Our Principal Is a Wolf!

Our Principal's in His Underwear!

Our Principal Breaks a Spell!

Our Principal's Wacky Wishes!

The Adventures of Allie and Amy
By Stephanie Calmenson and Joanna Cole

Book 1: *The Best Friend Plan*

Book 2: *Rockin' Rockets*

Book 3: *Stars of the Show*

Our Principal
Is a Spider!

BY
Stephanie
Calmenson

ILLUSTRATED
BY Aaron
Blecha

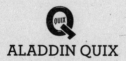

ALADDIN QUIX

New York London Toronto Sydney New Delhi

To Noah, with love
—S. C.

This book is a work of fiction. Any references to historical events, real people, or real places are used fictitiously. Other names, characters, places, and events are products of the author's imagination, and any resemblance to actual events or places or persons, living or dead, is entirely coincidental.

ALADDIN QUIX
Simon & Schuster Children's Publishing Division
1230 Avenue of the Americas, New York, New York 10020
First Aladdin QUIX paperback edition February 2021
Text copyright © 2021 by Stephanie Calmenson
Illustrations copyright © 2021 by Aaron Blecha
Also available in an Aladdin QUIX hardcover edition.
All rights reserved, including the right of reproduction in whole or in part in any form.
ALADDIN and the related marks and colophon are
trademarks of Simon & Schuster, Inc.
For information about special discounts for bulk purchases, please contact
Simon & Schuster Special Sales at 1-866-506-1949 or business@simonandschuster.com.
The Simon & Schuster Speakers Bureau can bring authors to your live event. For
more information or to book an event contact the Simon & Schuster Speakers Bureau
at 1-866-248-3049 or visit our website at www.simonspeakers.com.
Designed by Karin Paprocki
The illustrations for this book were rendered digitally.
The text of this book was set in Archer Medium.
Manufactured in the United States of America 0121 OFF
2 4 6 8 10 9 7 5 3 1
Library of Congress Control Number 2020943654
ISBN 978-1-5344-5759-1 (hc)
ISBN 978-1-5344-5758-4 (pbk)
ISBN 978-1-5344-5760-7 (ebook)

Cast of Characters

Mr. Barnaby Bundy: Principal

Marty Q. Marvel: Bumbling magician

Anansi (also known as Mr. Araknid): Tricky spider

Ms. Marilyn Moore: Assistant principal

Ms. Ellie Tilly: Kindergarten teacher

Hector Gonzalez: Loves making his friends laugh

Roger Patel: A top student and class leader

Nancy Wong: Plans to be a zoologist

Ms. Wanda Bly: Gym teacher

Mr. Charles Strong: School librarian

Mr. Joseph Klein: Science teacher

Ms. Gretta Sharp (also known as Seven): Magician and granddaughter of the famous magician named Five

Contents

Chapter 1: A Banner Day 1

Chapter 2: *Poof!* 7

Chapter 3: Who'll Be Next? 15

Chapter 4: Bye-Bye, Ms. Bly 21

Chapter 5: So Long, Mr. Strong 30

Chapter 6: A Plan 39

Chapter 7: Gretta Sharp 50

Chapter 8: Seven Ate Nine 56

Chapter 9: Look Who's Back 62

Word List 69

Questions 72

1

A Banner Day

Mr. Bundy, the principal of PS 88, was whistling a happy tune as he pedaled to school on his bike.

He was proud his students had won top prizes at the district Math Meet. It was a ten-out-of-ten morning!

While he was pedaling, he was planning a special assembly to celebrate his teachers' and students' accomplishments.

I could invite **Marty Q. Marvel,** *the magician,* thought Mr. Bundy. He stopped to **reconsider.** *No, I'd better not. I like Marty, but his tricks rarely work.*

While Mr. Bundy was trying to come up with a better idea, he didn't notice the spider racing across the handlebars of his bike, then jumping off.

He *did* notice the man who popped out in front of him on the road.

"Good morning!" the man called. "Are you Mr. Bundy, the principal of PS 88?"

Mr. Bundy stopped short.

"Why, yes, I am," said Mr. Bundy. "May I help you?"

"Thanks, but I'm here to help *you!*" said the man.

"Really? How?" asked Mr. Bundy.

"My name is **Mr. Araknid**," said the man. "I understand congratulations are in order!"

He explained, "I read about

PS 88's excellent performance at the Math Meet, and I thought you might be interested in celebration banners for schools with high accomplishments."

"**What a good idea!** My teachers and students definitely deserve a celebration banner," said Mr. Bundy. "Can you come to my office this afternoon?"

"I'm busy this afternoon," the man **fibbed**. "But if you've got a couple of minutes, I can show you some of the banners right now."

"Sure, why not?" said Mr. Bundy.

The answer to that question was just moments away.

Mr. Bundy had no idea he was speaking to a tricky spider named **Anansi**, who had magically **transformed** himself into a man. Unlike Marty Q. Marvel, Anansi's tricks never failed.

2

Poof!

"So, how many banners would you like?" asked the man.

"One large one will be plenty," said Mr. Bundy.

"Sounds good," said the man. "I'll show you my four favorites, and you can choose the one you like best."

He fanned out a selection of banners for Mr. Bundy to see.

"They all look very nice," said Mr. Bundy. "But as the principal of the school that placed so well at the Math Meet, I have to correct you. There aren't four banners here. There are five."

POOF!

As soon as Mr. Bundy said "five," there was a burst of bright-colored

smoke. When the smoke cleared,
Mr. Bundy was gone!

Anansi's face lit up as he sang
to himself:

"He said 'five' loud and
clear,
and I made the principal
disappear!
Ha, ha, ha! Ho, ho, ho!
It was fun to make him go!"

Anansi had learned the disappearing trick from a very tiny, very old woman who had magic powers. Her name was Five, and she hated her name because people made fun of it.

So whenever anyone said it, she

used her magic powers to make them disappear.

But Five had been no match for Anansi. **He learned *her* trick, then made her disappear!**

Now Mr. Bundy was gone and only Anansi knew where to find him.

For his next sneaky trick, Anansi went into Mr. Bundy's backpack and pulled out his phone.

He quickly checked the address book and found a listing for the assistant principal of PS

88. Her name was **Ms. Moore**.

"If I send a message from the principal's phone, Ms. Moore will think it came from Mr. Bundy." Anansi chuckled to himself.

"I'll make sure to give her a good reason why the principal can't come to school today. I'll give her an even better reason why I should be the school's special visitor. And what a special visitor I'll be!"

He quickly texted a message as if it were coming from Mr. Bundy:

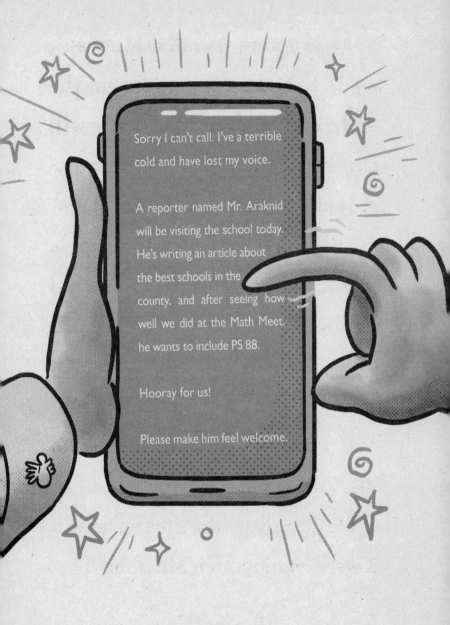

Sorry I can't call. I've a terrible cold and have lost my voice.

A reporter named Mr. Araknid will be visiting the school today. He's writing an article about the best schools in the county, and after seeing how well we did at the Math Meet, he wants to include PS 88.

Hooray for us!

Please make him feel welcome.

Anansi was quite pleased with what he'd written and thought **"Hooray for us!"** was an extra-nice touch.

He hit "send," then hopped onto Mr. Bundy's bicycle. His exciting day of mischief was just getting started.

3

Who'll Be Next?

A short distance from the school, Anansi hid behind a row of bushes.

When all the students and teachers had gone in, he left Mr. Bundy's bike hidden and made his entrance.

Ms. Moore was at the door waiting to greet latecomers.

"Good morning!" called Anansi. "I'm Mr. Araknid and I believe Mr. Bundy told you I'd be visiting today." He put his spidery fingers together and bowed his greeting.

"Welcome to PS 88!" said Ms. Moore. "Come in and I'll introduce you to our teachers and students."

"Thank you for inviting me in, but no introduction is needed,"

said Anansi. "I'd like to just quietly observe a typical day."

And make a few teachers disappear, thought the tricky spider.

He did not mention that he was a man—or, rather, a spider—on a mission. He'd be making the teachers disappear for a good cause and was sure everyone would understand if he ever had the chance to explain.

"I'll just announce that you're visiting with us," said Ms. Moore.

"It will be best not to mention that I'm a reporter. It makes some people nervous," said Anansi.

"No problem," said Ms. Moore. "I'll show you where my office is and give you my number in case you have a question."

Anansi thanked Ms. Moore and went off to find the best teachers for his secret plan. Soon, he heard Ms. Moore's voice over the loud-speaker.

"Good morning, teachers and students. I'm sorry to report that Mr. Bundy is home today with a bad cold. I'm sure everyone wishes him a speedy recovery. In other news, we have a special visitor with us. His name is Mr. Araknid. Please welcome him if you see him, and have an excellent PS 88 day."

Anansi walked happily down the hall, looking for the first teacher for his plan. His excellent PS 88 day had begun.

4

Bye-Bye, Ms. Bly

Walking along, Anansi heard the delightful voices of children singing.

"The itsy-bitsy spider climbed up the waterspout!

Down came the rain and washed the spider out!"

How nice. They're singing about spiders, thought Anansi as he followed the voices down the hall.

A sign on the door said MS. TILLY'S KINDERGARTEN. **Ms. Tilly** would be very helpful for his plan, but he didn't have the heart to leave these sweet young children teacherless.

Feeling proud of himself for his kindness, he danced away down the hall as they sang:

"Out came the sun and dried up all the rain. And the itsy-bitsy spider climbed up the spout again!"

I'd better not turn into a softie, he thought. He followed the sound of children's excited shouts to Room 105. The word GYM was spelled out in big letters at the top of the doorway.

"Yo, Hector! Pass the ball!" called a boy.

"Coming at you, **Roger!**"

answered Hector, throwing the basketball.

The ball didn't make it to Roger. It was **intercepted** by a girl, who dribbled it the other way down the court. When she got close enough to the basket, she took her shot. **Swish!**

"Yay, Nancy!" called her teammates.

Ms. Bly, the gym teacher, blew her whistle. "Game's over, kids. Time for your cooldown run."

The kids formed a line, ran twice around the gym, then filed out the door.

When they were gone, Anansi stepped inside, pretending to look confused.

"Hello," he said. "I'm Mr. Araknid, the visitor Ms. Moore mentioned, and I'm hoping you can help me."

"Of course," said Ms. Bly. "Welcome to PS 88."

"Thank you. I was looking for Room 104," said Anansi.

"Room 104's across the way," said Ms. Bly.

"Oh, what room am I in?" asked the sneaky man, knowing very well where he was.

Ms. Bly answered, "This room is 105."

POOF!

There was a burst of bright-colored smoke, and then the coach was gone.

"Bye-bye, Ms. Bly," chuckled Anansi. He did his little dance and sang:

"Ha, ha, ha! Ho, ho, ho!
It was fun to make her go!"

The magic trick he'd learned from old woman Five never failed. Anansi shivered with excitement over how well his plan was going.

When the teachers disappeared, they'd be reunited with Mr. Bundy, and Anansi would have them all just where he needed them.

Meanwhile, Anansi had no idea he was being watched from the

doorway of the gym. Roger had come back to get the water bottle he'd left behind. Seeing Ms. Bly disappear, his eyes popped. His jaw dropped.

No way! *This can't be,* Roger thought. He rubbed his eyes, hoping they were tricking him. But when he opened them again, Ms. Bly was still gone.

He ran to find his friends.

5

So Long, Mr. Strong

Roger's class was at the library. He was glad Hector and Nancy were sitting together.

"Pssst! Pssst!" he whispered. He led them to a corner and told them the story.

"Yeah, right," said Nancy. "The coach disappeared into thin air. **_POOF!_**"

"Exactly," said Roger.

"Did you get hit on the head by the basketball or something?" asked Hector.

"I wondered about that myself," said Roger.

Suddenly he gasped. The visitor was standing at the door. **Mr. Strong**, their beloved librarian, went to greet him.

Uh-oh! This could be trouble.

"We can't let Mr. Strong be alone with him," Roger said, sounding **frantic**.

Nancy reached up and felt Roger's forehead.

"What are you *doing*?" hissed Roger.

"I'm seeing if you have a fever. You sound **delirious**," said Nancy.

"I know what I saw. Or didn't see. I saw Ms. Bly and then I didn't," said Roger.

Suddenly the kids realized Mr. Strong and the visitor were gone.

Roger, Hector and Nancy slipped out of the library and followed the voices down the hall. Peeking around a corner, they had a clear view and could hear every word.

"So, Mr. Strong, how long

have you been at PS 88?" asked the visitor.

"Let me see. I think this is my fifth year," said the librarian.

"**Oh really?** I would have guessed at least six years," said Anansi.

"No," said Mr. Strong. "Just five."

POOF!

The moment Mr. Strong said the word "five," there was a burst of bright-colored smoke and he was gone.

The kids' eyes popped. Their jaws dropped.

They heard the visitor chuckle as he said, "So long, Mr. Strong."

He did his little dance and sang:

"Ha, ha, ha! Ho, ho, ho!
It was fun to make him go!"

"Now do you believe me?" said Roger in a strangled voice.

"I—I don't know," **stammered** Hector, checking his own forehead for a fever.

"I'm telling you," said Roger. "This is the second time someone talking to that man said 'five,' then disappeared."

"What are we going to do about it?" said Nancy.

Just then, the visitor looked their way.

Hector thought fast. He didn't want Mr. Araknid to know they saw what he just did. If he knew, he might make *them* disappear.

"Hi there, sir!" he called. "Have you seen Mr. Strong? We could use some help finding a book for our homework."

The man quickly put on a phony look of concern.

"Your librarian wasn't feeling well, so he went home," the spider said. "Stomach flu, I think."

"That's too bad," said Hector. "Thanks."

The three friends made their way back to the library, **trembling** from head to toe.

6

A Plan

"We need to call the police," said Nancy.

"Sure," said Roger. "I'll just say, 'Hello, officer. There's a man in our school who makes everyone disappear as soon as they say the word "five.'" Then, as soon as I finish, they'll arrest me for being a **prankster**."

"We'd better tell Ms. Moore," said Hector. "She'll believe us. We've done some wacky things at school, but we've never made up a story as crazy as this."

"You're right," said Nancy. **"Let's go!"**

They left the library and headed down the hallway to Ms. Moore's office. Ahead of them, the door to the stairwell was open and they could hear Mr. Araknid's voice.

"So, how do you like your new students?" he said.

"The little spiders are charming. But I must get back to PS 88!" said another voice.

The voice sounded like Mr. Bundy's! But he didn't sound one bit sick. He just sounded angry.

The kids inched closer to the stairwell so they could look in. Mr. Araknid had his back to them. He was holding up his phone, and they could see who was on the screen.

It looked a lot like Mr. Bundy, only it wasn't the Mr. Bundy they knew. **It was Spider Man Bundy!**

"You must stop this trickery and send Ms. Bly, Mr. Strong and me back at once!" demanded the principal.

"Sorry, no can do," said Mr. Araknid. "I want to make my Little Spiders School of Mischief to be a great success and you're just the people I need."

He added, "I want my students to be as smart as the students at PS 88. In fact, I'll be capturing a few more of your teachers very soon."

"Listen to me," said Mr. Bundy. "We wish your little spiders well, but we will refuse to teach them." Then he shouted, **"You must let us go!"**

The kids had never heard their principal raise his voice before. But **desperate** times call for desperate measures. Mr. Bundy's shout jump-started Nancy's brain.

"I can't believe I missed it!" she said.

"What? What did you miss?" said Roger.

Nancy planned to be a **zoologist** someday, and made it her business to know about the animal kingdom. She already knew lots about spiders. And she knew that a spider is an **arachnid**.

That's why he calls himself Mr. Araknid! thought Nancy.

She pulled her friends back from the stairway.

"That man is no man," said Nancy. "He's a tricky spider who transformed himself."

"That means he's Anansi!" said Hector. "Mr. Strong read us stories about him."

The kids heard the conversation in the stairwell coming to an end.

"You can help my little spiders be the best that they can be," said Anansi. "Or spend the rest of your lives spinning webs and eating insects. Goodbye."

When Anansi came out to the

hallway, the kids tried their best to not look nervous.

"Shouldn't you three be getting back to the library?" asked Anansi.

"Yes, sir," said Hector.

"On our way," said Roger.

"Here we go!" said Nancy.

When they got there, Roger said, "You two go in. I'm going to get help."

"Are you going to Ms. Moore?" asked Nancy.

"No. I'm afraid Anansi might get **suspicious** if he sees me talking to

Ms. Moore. I'm worried he'll make her disappear. He might even make *me* disappear," said Roger.

"Then who will you get?" said Hector.

"Believe it or not," said Roger, "I'm going to call Marty—"

"Q?" said Hector.

"Marvel?" said Nancy.

Everyone at PS 88 knew Marty Q. Marvel's motto: *My marvelous magic will amaze you!* The amazing thing was that his magic had never, ever worked.

"I know it's risky, but I think Marty will believe us," said Roger. "And I'll tell him it's a super-important, two-magician job."

"Good idea," said Nancy. "If we're lucky, he'll bring someone whose magic tricks actually work."

"Hurry," said Hector. "The first graders are heading for the Science Center, and Anansi's right behind them. He might go after **Mr. Klein**, the science teacher, next!"

7

Gretta Sharp

Roger slipped into Mr. Bundy's office. On the desk was a list of possible guests for a special assembly, and the magician's phone number was on it.

Luckily, when Roger called, Marty

answered right away. He listened carefully to Roger's story.

"I know just who to bring," said Marty. "We'll be there as soon as we can."

It wasn't soon enough! Nancy and Hector had each asked to be excused from class and went to join Roger. They told him that now Mr. Klein and Ms. Moore were missing too!

The three friends were starting to panic. If only Mr. Bundy were there, he'd know what to do.

They went to the front door of the school to wait for Marty's arrival. It wasn't long before he came tripping in, followed by a very tall young woman. A moment later, they saw Anansi hurrying down the hallway.

The young woman stepped forward and introduced herself. She knew very well who she was speaking to, but said, "Hello, sir. You must be Mr. Bundy. I'm **Gretta Sharp**, Mr. Marvel's talent agent. I hear you called yesterday about an assembly

program for your highly accomplished students and teachers."

"They certainly are accomplished, but I'm *not* Mr. Bundy. He's out sick today," said Anansi.

"Then we can see Ms. Moore," said Gretta Sharp.

"I'm afraid she went home sick too," said Anansi.

"And you are?" said Ms. Sharp.

"I'm Mr. Araknid. I was visiting for the day and was just leaving," he said, trying to slip away.

"I see. Did you come to meet

the students who **aced** the Math Meet?" asked Ms. Sharp, not letting him pass.

"Yes, they're wonderful, wonderful students!" said Anansi.

In the meantime, he was thinking, *There's something familiar and worrisome about this Ms. Sharp.*

8

Seven Ate Nine

Anansi tried to move past Gretta, but she was shifting like an athlete guarding the ball.

"Those students really are amazing," said Gretta. "I always found math a little scary." Then she added with a mischievous smile, "Can you guess which number I thought was the scariest?"

"I don't have to guess," said Anansi, trying again to get past her. "Everyone knows that joke. The scariest number is seven."

POOF!

As soon as he said "seven," there was a burst of bright-colored smoke. When it was gone, so was Anansi.

"Ha! Ha! Ha! Ho! Ho! Ho! I tricked Anansi and I made him go!" chanted Gretta. "That silly spider never even made it to the end of the joke, so the joke's on him. The scariest number is seven because..."

"Seven ate nine!" called Roger, Nancy and Hector together.

"You did it! You got rid of him!" said Roger.

"Thank you!" said Nancy.

"By the way, who *are* you?" asked Hector.

Gretta threw off her cape and wig and jumped down from her stilts. What a surprise! She was not tall at all. In fact, she was tiny.

Anansi had no idea who he'd been talking to. Gretta explained.

"My real name is **Seven**," she said. "Marty and I met at the

Presto-Chango School of Magic. My family has been going there for generations. Maybe you've heard of my famous grandmother, Five. She could make anyone who said her name disappear. Her trick became a family secret."

"I knew it!" said Roger. "Anyone Anansi got to say 'five' disappeared. Now anyone who says . . ." He stopped before saying the number seven.

"Don't worry," said Gretta. "You're safe. I only trick troublemakers."

"Why were you wearing stilts?" asked Roger.

"I look a lot like my dear grandma, who was tiny. I wanted to look very different from her so Anansi wouldn't recognize me," said Seven.

Then Nancy asked the most important question of all.

"Can you bring our principals and teachers back?" she said.

"I can," said Seven. "But I'm going to give Marty the honor. Ready, Marty?"

"Sure thing!" said Marty.

9

Look Who's Back

The kids looked worried as Marty chanted, **"One, two, five, seven and nine. All come back now, feeling fine!"**

Nothing happened.

"That's odd," said Marty.

"Actually, one of the numbers is *not* odd," said Seven. "Do you really want to include *two* in your list of odd numbers?"

"Hmm," said Marty, tapping his chin. "Oh, I get it!" He tried again.

"One, *three*, five, seven and nine. All come back now, feeling fine!"

POOF!

There was a burst of bright-colored smoke, and when it was gone, Mr. Bundy, Ms. Moore, Ms. Bly, Mr. Strong and Mr. Klein were back. Thankfully, they were not spiders anymore.

Mr. Bundy brushed off his suit and straightened his tie.

"Thank you, both," he said to the magicians. **"It's good to be back**

at PS 88! I hope you'll agree to be the special guests at our upcoming Math Meet celebration."

The magicians said they'd be honored.

• • •

Three days later, Marty Q. Marvel and Seven put on a memorable magic show. In a thrilling **finale**, Gretta turned Mr. Bundy back into a spider, then made him disappear.

It took Marty quite a few tries to bring Mr. Bundy back, but in the end, he did himself proud. He was smiling from ear to ear as the kids and teachers gave the magicians their best even-numbered cheer:

"Two, four, six, eight!

Who do we appreciate?

Marty! Seven!

Hooray!"

There was one last burst of bright-colored smoke, and then the magicians disappeared from the stage.

POOF!

Word List

aced (AYST): Did something extremely well

arachnid (uh•RAK•nihd): A member of the class of animals that includes spiders, scorpions, mites and ticks

delirious (dih•LEER•ee•us): In a confused mental state

desperate (DEH•spuh•ret): Having a complete loss of hope

fibbed (FIBD): Told a small lie

finale (fih•NA•lee): The end of something

frantic (FRAN•tik): Having nervous feelings that are out of control

intercepted (in•ter•SEP•ted): Stopped and caught something on its way somewhere

prankster (PRANK•ster): A person who plays tricks

reconsider (ree•kuhn•SIH•der): To think about something again, especially for a possible change of mind

stammered (STA•merd):
Stumbled over words

suspicious (suh•SPIH•shus):
Thinking something might be
wrong, maybe without having
proof

transformed (trans•FORMD):
Changed the form or appearance
of something or someone

trembling (TREM•bling):
Shaking from nerves or
excitement

zoologist (zoh•AH•luh•jist): A
scientist who studies animals

Questions

1. If you were worried about a stranger at school, who would you call for help? (Hint: The answer is *not* Marty Q. Marvel.)

2. Do you know the story of "Anansi and the Yam Hills"? If not, have fun reading it, and then see how it's the same and how it's different from this story.

3. If you had a chance to be the teacher of little spiders, what would you teach them and why?